A TALE OF
TWO PONIES

OR

Who's the Cutest
Pony in the Barn?

By Linda Vital

ACKNOWLEDGEMENTS

I would like to thank all my friends who encouraged me in my plan to write my second book. My husband and children were again enthusiastic about yet another of my many projects.

Nancy Dickie and Sandy Ruch were diligent proof-readers for me. Sandy Ruch's wonderful appendix appears here once more, and my daughter, Liz, delighted me with her very creative article about Shetland ponies.

I would like to express my love and thanks to Nick Coyne and Kristi Horwitz, the leaders of our program at Horsefeathers. They are building a haven for the challenged people of all ages. This book is for them and all the volunteers and supporters that make it all possible.

Most of all, I salute our horses, who work hard and bring smiles to so many. Like the silly ponies in my story, they all have feelings that they put aside every day when they are called upon to do their jobs. They are our silent partners in our endeavor to make this world a better place.

To order additional copies of this book, contact:
Xlibris Corporation
1-888-795-4274
www.Xlibris.com
Orders@Xlibris.com

DEDICATION

For Benny, who tried so hard…

For Simon, who didn't have to…

And for all the people who saved me.

CHAPTER ONE

"They were the best of ponies, they were the worst of ponies!"

This is a tale of two ponies named L'il Sugar and Hollywood. They were not just ordinary ponies. They belonged to a very special breed of horses called Shetland Ponies. These ponies come from the Shetland Islands in Scotland, where it is quite cold. Because it is so cold there, the ponies grow thick, fuzzy coats, which not only keep them nice and warm, but also make them look very cute. Besides being very cute, L'il Sugar and Hollywood were also very smart, which you will soon find out.

L'il Sugar and Hollywood worked together at a barn called Happy Trails. At this barn, people of all ages learned to ride horses. Most of the riders were children who were mentally or physically challenged. Some had muscles that didn't work well; some couldn't walk on their own at all. Others had trouble concentrating on tasks. At Happy Trails, the one thing they could all do was learn to ride and have fun!

People from all over knew of Happy Trails and the wonderful horses who worked there. The most well-known of them all was Bud. Happy Trails had become his new home after he retired from the Chicago Mounted Police Unit, and he was beloved by all. The children loved him and all the other horses and ponies looked up to him.

L'il Sugar and Hollywood were quite enamored with Bud, as were many of the other mares! Each of them truly believed he liked her best.

Now, I must tell you that we really can't say that our two dear ponies worked "together." Although they were well-trained, hard-working ponies, they were not really very good friends. They did not socialize with each other at all. They were both very, very cute, as Shetland Ponies usually are. They had beautiful markings and long, fluffy tails and thick, flowing manes. Everyone who came to the barn just raved about how unbelievably CUTE they were! They were showered with attention.

This is where the problem came in. How can a barn exist with TWO cute ponies, without ONE of them wanting to be the CUTEST !?!?

CHAPTER TWO

Now, it has been stated that besides being very cute, L'il Sugar and Hollywood were also very smart. As you remember, they were SHETLAND PONIES from Scotland! They were always thinking! At least, they looked like they were, although what was actually going on inside those cute, fuzzy heads of theirs was anybody's guess!

As the author of this book, I happen to have some rare insight into those little pony-minds. I will tell you that most of their thoughts revolved around who was the cutest pony in the barn, and whether or not one was outdoing the other!

Happy Trails was a very busy place. Besides the weekly lessons, there were always other fun things going on. There were parties and horse shows and people coming to visit - lots of opportunities for horses and humans to join together and have fun......OR be rivals!!!!!! During these times, L'il Sugar and Hollywood each tried her best to be the center of attention.

CHAPTER THREE

From the last chapter you might possibly get the impression that L'il Sugar and Hollywood were two very horrid, self-absorbed ponies indeed. I am happy to say that this, my friends, could not be further from the truth.

When it came to doing their jobs, they were outstanding, perfectly behaved little ponies. They both loved their work! They never complained about walking round and round the arena - sometimes hungry, hot or tired. They always soldiered on like good little troopers. They loved the children dearly. They didn't even mind getting called to do a lesson as the hay wagon arrived! It was "Duty First" with our little Shetlanders….their Scottish ancestors would have been proud of them! They never caused trouble for the other horses, nor were they bossy with any of the other mares.

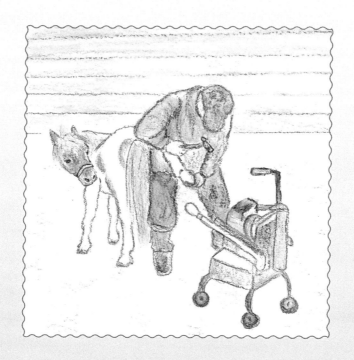

Most important of all, for any horse, is that they always co-operated with the farrier. The farrier is the person who takes care of the horses' hooves. There's nothing more ill-mannered than a horse that tries to kick the farrier! L'il Sugar and Hollywood always stood perfectly still while being fitted for their new shoes. Of course, it only made sense to do this, as this way they always got very pretty shoes!

CHAPTER FOUR

So you can see that L'il Sugar and Hollywood, despite their rivalry, managed to live in relative peace with each other most of the time. For one thing, besides being from the Shetland Islands in Scotland, they also happened to both be from the same clan, which was quite fortunate.

They each had their own special friends, and their stalls were not near each other, so there were not too many opportunities for them to get on each others' nerves.

If only the lady from the newspaper had not come, everything would have been just fine! That is exactly what did happen, however, and let me tell you, the consequences were dire! One of the little riders at Happy Trails happened to have a neighbor who worked for the local newspaper, and she told her all about the place. The woman decided to write a human interest story for the paper. She came one day with a photographer to do the story, using her little neighbor as the central character. She would write an article about the little girl's lesson, and have pictures of her on her favorite pony.

CHAPTER FIVE

Well, dear friends, L'il Sugar was the pony that the little girl usually rode, but by a quirk of fate, Sugar had just had pretty new shoes put on that morning. Her feet had to have a rest. When she learned that she was going to miss out on being the Star of the Day, with her picture in the paper, she was just heart-broken!

When the reporter, the photographer, and the little girl showed up, they passed right by L'il Sugar's stall. They were so busy talking they did not even stop by to say hello. The little girl even forgot to give her a pat as she went by. This was very hard for our L'il Sugar to bear.

They headed straight for Hollywood's stall. "Hollywood, L'il Sugar cannot work today. How would you like to do my lesson with me and have your picture in the newspaper?" asked the little girl. "We can both be famous together!"

Hollywood's ears perked up when she heard this! "Wow, this is my lucky day!" thought Hollywood. "What a shame my friend, L'il Sugar, will miss out on the fun." She chuckled inside.

As the little girl and Hollywood went out to the arena, they passed by L'il Sugar's stall and saw that she was way back in the corner with her back turned, her head hanging low.

L'il Sugar did not want to see them walk by, and she did not want them to see that she was crying.

Hollywood felt a little badly for L'il Sugar, but not terribly so. After all, they did have that little rivalry going, and SHE was going to be in the newspaper! People would read about HER and see HER picture and think that SHE was the cutest pony in the barn! Who could blame her for being a wee bit excited!

The lesson and interviews and picture-taking went well, and the next day several people had brought in copies of the morning paper. "Look! There's our girl on the front page!" one of the volunteers exclaimed. They hung copies of the article and pictures of Hollywood all over the barn.

Poor L'il Sugar. Everywhere she went, she had to see pictures of Hollywood and her little rider. She wondered if her little girl would ever want to ride with her again. She was very sad.

CHAPTER SIX

AND MAD !!!!!!

"How could Hollywood steal my rider and then be famous in the newspaper and everything?!!! She must think she is quite special now!" thought L'il Sugar.

The more she thought about the whole thing, the madder she got. "What if she steals all of my other riders and becomes even more famous and they decide to send me away forever?" she thought.

And then, when she thought that she couldn't possibly get any madder ....

the most UNBEARABLE thought in the entire world occurred to her.....

"What if people think that Hollywood is the cutest pony in the barn?"

CHAPTER SEVEN

What happened next can only be described as outrageous. L'il Sugar's poor pony-brain was clouded with jealousy and dismay. She decided to do an unspeakable thing! She watched as one of the volunteers went into Hollywood's stall to put her saddle on.

"C'mon, Hollywood, another rider for you. You sure are one busy girl lately," he said as he led her out to the arena.

As L'il Sugar watched Hollywood walk by, she made her move. Remember that I said that Shetland Ponies were not only very cute, but that they also were very smart?

Well, they also could be very sneaky! Our crafty, naughty L'il Sugar had been practicing a new trick every night; she had learned to un-latch her stall door!

As soon as Hollywood had gone around the corner, out strolled L'il Sugar. She tip-toed as quietly as she could (which is not easy for an animal with hooves and metal shoes!) right into Hollywood's stall and saw exactly what she wanted right away. She started gobbling up Hollywood's hay, as fast as she could, every single bite of it.

"Hollywood won't be able to do all those lessons if she is hungry now, will she!?" exclaimed L'il Sugar. She left a few strands of hay just to torment Hollywood. Imagine having just ONE potato chip to eat? She cautiously stuck her head outside the stall door to make sure the coast was clear. She deftly made her way back to her own stall, and was pleased to see that her own pile of hay was waiting there for her. It was kind of like having dessert!

L'il Sugar was indeed quite pleased with herself, and wondered how long it would take for her plan to have an effect. From then on, she took every opportunity she could to sneak in and gorge herself on Hollywood's food.

CHAPTER EIGHT

Well, our friend, Hollywood, was such a hard worker that it didn't take long for her to start to suffer from lack of food! Her little stomach growled all the time, and she started to get light-headed. People noticed her dragging her feet during lessons, and she wasn't able to give her riders a nice trot at all.

Don, one of the volunteers, noticed that something just wasn't quite right with Hollywood. "Her head is hanging low and her eyes have lost their sparkle. And look how skinny she is." he said.

The other volunteers agreed and they had the boss call the vet. The vet came and looked at her. He agreed that she was indeed losing weight. Don said, "But she always eats all her food. There's never so much as a scrap left in her stall after the grooms have fed her." Of course, no one ever even imagined that someone could have been so dishonorable as to steal her food! Who would have suspected that it was a horse committing the crime! No one knew how smart AND sneaky Shetland Ponies could be!

CHAPTER NINE

"Well," said the vet. "I think we'll have to bring Hollywood to the Horse Hospital and check her out. She's fading away, poor girl!"

Hollywood felt so miserable, and she was very scared. All the volunteers walked out with her and patted her and consoled her. "Don't worry, Hollywood, they'll fix you up and you'll be as good as new. And we'll all come visit you in the hospital," said Don.

L'il Sugar peeked out her stall door as the procession went by. Our spiteful little pony was actually jealous about all the attention Hollywood was getting!

L'il Sugar watched as they gently led Hollywood into the trailer. The vet rolled slowly away from the barn, to deliver Hollywood to the Horse Hospital.

CHAPTER TEN

"Well, if Hollywood is no longer here, I guess it will just be a matter of time before I am declared the Cutest Pony in the Barn!" thought L'il Sugar, gleefully.

While Hollywood was away, L'il Sugar had to take over a lot of her work. She did it willingly, as always. In fact, she was eager to show everyone how wonderful she was.

She did a good job, and was highly rewarded with praise and treats. Most of Hollywood's riders started to ride L'il Sugar now, and she was thrilled. One day, she heard one of the riders say that she was starting to like L'il Sugar better than Hollywood.

"She probably thinks I'm much cuter than Hollywood as well!" she exclaimed.

As the days went on, L'il Sugar was happy and busy, but she often heard people talking about Hollywood. They said they missed her, and wondered how she was doing. At first, L'il Sugar did not care at all to hear how Hollywood was doing, but after awhile, she started to get curious about her.

"Hollywood has been away for quite awhile. I wonder how she is doing, after all," thought L'il Sugar.

CHAPTER ELEVEN

L'il Sugar actually started to feel kind of lonely.....even a little sad at times. This in spite of the fact that she had many riders that loved her, and everyone thought highly of her for taking on Hollywood's work. "Don't' worry, L'il Sugar. Before you know it, Hollywood will be back and you'll get to rest a little." said Don one day.

Now, the L'il Sugar of old would not have liked to hear that said, because she would be worrying about Hollywood getting more attention than her again. However, something had changed in L'il Sugar, and she was a bit confused about her feelings. Even though Shetland Ponies are very smart, they don't quite understand themselves when they start to get emotional - it's just not in their nature! L'il Sugar started becoming very anxious.

She decided to go where all the other horses (and sometimes humans) went when they were troubled - to see Bud, the wise old retired police horse. Bud had worked for many years on the beat in Chicago, and joined Happy Trails when he was retired from the Mounted Police Unit. Besides being a great favorite of the riders, he was well-loved by all the other horses. He enjoyed helping anyone and everyone with their problems. He said his stall door was always open for those who needed two fuzzy ears to listen to them.

31

CHAPTER TWELVE

L'il Sugar stood outside Bud's stall for more than a few minutes trying to think of what to say. As was mentioned before, Shetland Ponies are very stoic little individuals, not given to talk much about their inner feelings. She had no idea how to approach Bud.

Luckily, Bud had just finished his breakfast and was turning himself around to stick his head out of his stall window to see what was going on out in the world that day. He looked down to see a glum little pony lurking outside his door. "Well, fancy meeting you here, L'il Sugar! Top o'the morning to you!" he happily exclaimed.

Faced with such cheerfulness, especially so early in the morning, Sugar felt even worse. "Well, it may be the top o'the morning to you, Bud, but it surely isn't to me!" she said.

Though he was a bit taken aback by this rebuff, Bud realized right away that something was very wrong with his little pal. He immediately gave her a friendly nicker and asked what was bothering her. His kind manner melted her heart and she easily poured out her troubles to him.

L'il Sugar admitted her terrible deed and her strong desire to be the cutest pony in the barn, but said that now she missed her friend and was sorry she hurt her. She said she wanted very badly to go visit Hollywood at the Horse Hospital and help her get better. She even wanted to tell Hollywood that SHE could be the cutest pony in the barn forever and ever. She said she wanted to be a much nicer pony from now on and could Bud please think of a way to help her do all these things?

Well, as shocked as Bud was after hearing such a confession, he did not speak a word of reproach to L'il Sugar. He believed she was truly sorry and he felt very bad for her, as she was quite shaken up - a very sad state for a proud Shetland Pony to be in, to be sure.

So he just stood there and thought and thought. He believed that this was a good thing to do before offering any kind of pronouncement. He bent down and picked up a few strands of leftover hay from his breakfast, and he chewed for a few minutes. Chewing on hay always seemed to help him to think better.

"Gosh, well, being a horse and all, and a male horse at that," he said, "I haven't had too much experience wondering whether I'm cuter than any other horse, or whether I'm cute at all, for that matter. I guess I'm just lucky to be that way. Seems like that kind of thinking can get a horse in trouble!"

He chewed some more, and thought some more, and then continued. "You're not such a bad pony, L'il Sugar. Everyone knows that Shetland Ponies can be.....er..... a little difficult at times."

"Crabby! Downright crabby!" said Sugar.

"Okay, crabby, if you will. However, crabs are not bad animals. They, too, have a purpose. In fact, there are NO bad animals, all over this entire earth. We are all different and we just need to figure out what we need to do, and then just be nice to each other. It's really quite simple.

You and Hollywood need to form a team and work on your purpose together. How's this for an idea? I'm putting you in charge of Hollywood's Welcome Home Party. How would that be !!!!!" L'il Sugar liked that idea immediately. "Thanks, Bud. You have been a great help, as always. Now I must skedaddle - I have much to do!"

CHAPTER THIRTEEN

Next L'il Sugar decided to go to the Horse Hospital and see Hollywood to make amends. Don't ask me how she got there. We have learned that besides being very cute and smart, Shetland Ponies can also be very sneaky! So how she got there is not important.

What is important is that she found her way there, sneaked in the back door, and tip-toed in that quiet, clever way of hers, right down the hallway of the Sick Pony Section. She found Hollywood very easily. She just followed her heart. She walked up to the window of Hollywood's room.

L'il Sugar saw a crowd in the room with Hollywood. There were nurses and visitors all around her, patting her and singing to her and treating her like a queen. When Sugar saw this scene, she started to cry big, wet horse-tears.

Now, knowing the Sugar of old, you might think she was just being a jealous little pony, crying because she wanted all that attention lavished upon herself! However, this was a new L'il Sugar. She was so glad to see her friend, and she thought that being sick in the hospital was not the best way of getting attention. L'il Sugar felt so badly that she had been such a naughty pony!

One of the nurses saw her crying, and wondered what on earth a pony was doing out in the hall. When she saw those big horse-tears, she ran out and gave Sugar a hug, and told her to come in.

Hollywood was overjoyed to see Sugar; in fact, she was so happy she jumped right out of bed! "See?" said the nurse. "She was feeling so much better already and look at her now that she's seen her friend! She'll be able to go home in no time!"

Everyone left so L'il Sugar and Hollywood could have some time alone. Right away, L'il Sugar confessed her awful deed to Hollywood, even though she worried that Hollywood might never want to speak to her again. She needn't have worried, as horses are known to be the most forgiving of animals.

"L'il Sugar," Hollywood said, "don't you worry about the past. We were both much too busy worrying about who was the cutest pony in the barn, weren't we? We forgot about all the important things going on, like doing our work and just being friends. I am feeling much better now, so when I get back, we can just start all over and put all this behind us."

"Thank you so much for being so nice to me," said L'il Sugar. "Now I must go and tell everyone you will be back soon. They will all be so happy to have you come home."

L'il Sugar gave Hollywood a kiss good-bye and galloped all the way back to the barn, overjoyed. She thought about the Welcome Home Party the whole way home.

CHAPTER FOURTEEN

L'il Sugar told all the horses in the barn the good news, that Hollywood was all right and would be home soon. They were all very happy to hear it, and none of them wondered how L'il Sugar happened to have that information. They knew that Shetland Ponies were very smart and very sneaky, and somehow L'il Sugar had managed to get out and see Hollywood with none of them noticing.

L'il Sugar threw herself into her new project, which was to plan the grandest welcome-home party ever. About a week later, it was time for the big day. Sugar had done a great job planning the party, with a little help from the humans. Everyone was invited - riders, parents, volunteers, instructors, and of course all the horses and ponies and barn animals.

Outside the barn, there was a big sign with Hollywood's name on it and all kinds of decorations. It was a beautiful sunny day and there was to be a cook-out with lots of good things to eat.

The crowd gathered late in the morning. Hollywood was expected to arrive in her trailer around noon. The closer it got to noon, the more excited everyone became. No one was more excited than L'il Sugar. She was so nervous, she just paced back and forth, back and forth. She so wanted everything to be perfect!

Ever-thoughtful Bud saw her and went over to keep her company. "Well, Sugar, this will sure be a fun day, won't it? " he said. "I should say so," answered Sugar. "And I have a big surprise for Hollywood that I made for her myself!"

"Well my goodness, that sure is nice of you!" exclaimed Bud. "I didn't know you were creative." "Oh yes. We Shetland Ponies are not only cute and smart. We also happen to be quite creative." she said.

"And don't forget crabby! " laughed Bud. Sugar laughed too and added "and don't forget sneaky!"

CHAPTER FIFTEEN

All of a sudden, the trailer appeared at the end of the driveway. "Here she comes!" someone shouted.

The trailer pulled into the barn driveway and parked out next to the arena. Everyone lined up to wait for Hollywood to come out of her trailer. When she was led out, her heart leapt for joy. There were all her friends, humans and horses, waiting to greet her. The humans were all cheering and the horses were all running around madly in the arena, neighing and kicking up their heels!

L'il Sugar and Bud were not running around, though. They were just standing there with bright eyes and big horsey smiles. L'il Sugar had a few of those big horse-tears in her eyes. She had decided to let the humans and the other horses greet Hollywood first.

Hollywood had other ideas. She nudged the boy leading her in his back, letting him know that she wanted to go see Sugar right away. Shetland Ponies are not only cute and smart and creative and sneaky and crabby, they are also very persistent! She nearly dragged that boy over to the arena and kicked the gate with her hoof, demanding to be let in with the horses. The boy gladly went along with her wishes; after all, she was the star of the day!

As Hollywood passed through the gate, all the horses stopped running and they cleared a big space for her, and she nickered to L'il Sugar.

"Get over here, Sugar, this party is for both of us!" she said. L'il Sugar trotted right over to her friend and they gave each other a big hug. Bud joined them, and all the other horses started running around them in a big circle.

After a few minutes, Bud nickered to two of the big horses, Ice and Scatman. They ran off to the corner of the arena and picked something up off the ground. As they held it up, you could see that it was a big banner made out of grass and daisy-chains. These had been artfully knitted together by a certain little pony named L'il Sugar. On it were the words, "THE CUTEST OF ALL!"

L'il Sugar asked the two horses to drape the beautiful banner over Hollywood's back, and Hollywood walked around in a circle, proudly displaying it. Suddenly she stopped and looked at L'il Sugar. Then she walked over to Bud and asked him to put his head down so she could whisper in his ear. He nodded his head and gave a loud whinny and called for L'il Sugar to come join them.

Everyone watched as Bud picked up one side of the banner and draped it around L'il Sugar's shoulders.

"There you go," he said. "Who says a barn cannot exist with TWO cute ponies without one of them wanting to be the CUTEST?!" L'il Sugar and Hollywood looked at each other and nickered in agreement.

All the horses started running around again. The humans had their cook-out and played games and posed to have their pictures taken with the TWO cutest ponies in the barn.

CHAPTER SIXTEEN

As the sun set, the riders and their parents went home. The remaining humans put the tired and happy horses to bed. Believe it or not, after such a perfect day, there remained one more nice surprise.

It had been decided by some wise person that Hollywood might recuperate faster if she could move into a bigger stall, and have her friend live with her. Imagine Sugar and Hollywood's surprise as they were led down the aisle together, to see this magnificent new stall waiting for them! They couldn't believe their eyes! When they walked inside, they saw two big piles of hay and a whole pile of carrots and apples left over from the party for them to share.

Bud's stall was right across from them. He just had to chuckle as he watched them settling into their new home.

"Those Shetland Ponies sure are funny," he thought. "All that fuss and bother, just because both wanted to be the cutest pony in the barn. I'm sure glad I never worried about that kind of stuff. Actually, now that I think of it, though, I DO think I'M pretty cute. I just may even be the cutest boy horse in the barn!"

He bent his head down, chewed on some hay, and thought and thought.

He chewed some more hay, thought some more, then smiled a great big horsey smile.

Then he went to sleep.

Horses and Healing

written by Sandy Synnestvedt Ruch

Since antiquity, the horse and human bond has been known for its healing power. Use of the horse in a therapeutic role, from helping wounded veterans regain functionality, to augmenting the development of struggling children, has grown dramatically since the mid-twentieth century. Two principal programs have developed, which may appear similar from a distance, but have different focus:

Hippotherapy, i.e., treatment with help of the horse (from the Greek "hippo" meaning horse) is conducted by specially trained physical, occupational, and speech therapists who use the rhythmic, multi-dimensional motion of the horse as a treatment tool. Aided by a horse handler, the therapist directs the movement of the horse to influence the "rider", who may be positioned in various ways on the horse. The front-to-back, side-to-side movement of the horse closely simulates the movement that a person's body experiences in walking, and can have a powerful effect on individuals who have a movement dysfunction.

Therapeutic riding is taught by registered instructors who have been certified by NARHA, the North American Riding for the Handicapped Association. In this program, riders learn to control the horse and develop as much independence as they are able. In contrast to "hippo," here the rider is learning horsemanship - and still benefiting from the movement and energy of the horse. Whatever support the riders need, whether leading the horse or walking alongside to stabilize their position in the saddle, is provided by specially trained volunteers.

The program for each rider is customized to the specific objectives tailored to his/her ability. Second only to emphasis on safety is a large dose of fun - stretching, reaching, throwing, laughing all help the rider to relax, engage, and improve. Sessions may include games - throwing bean bags, shooting baskets, "red light green light," Simon Says - to develop coordination, focus attention, and interject fun, as appropriate for the individual's needs, maturity, and functionality.

In the hippotherapy and therapeutic ricling programs, we see individuals with a wide range of disabilities, including

1   Physical Disabilities

2   Cognitive Disabilities

3   Behavioral Challenges

4   Emotional Challenges

5   Attention Disorders

6   Autism Spectrum Disorders

Benefits that riders experience may include:

1   Increased muscle strength and tone

2   Increased balance and mobility

3   Increased range of motion

4   Improved confidence and self esteem

5   Greater ability to focus and stay on task

6   Behavioral improvements

7   Increased problem solving ability

Although physical and developmental benefits are numerous, there are intangible, even sweeter, benefits as well. Picture a wheelchair-bound child, accustomed to looking up at the world, being able to see the world from atop a horse, even learning how to direct this large animal; it is hugely empowering, and leaves the rider feeling "on top of the world."

 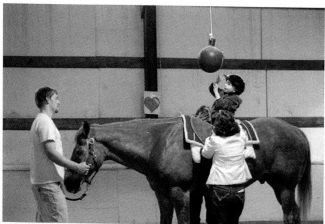

Biography

Sandra Ruch

For as long as I can remember, I've loved horses. And now, retired, I feel like the luckiest person in the world, spending every day with the horses and ponies who work their magic in a therapeutic program for riders with special needs.

My first contact with therapeutic riding was 10 years ago, as an intern working toward an Equine Science degree. Here I began to see what I had long sensed: a connection between horses and healing. In that internship, my mentor shared these words with me:

The strongest and the bravest are the kindest and the gentlest to the neediest.

Each day I see this borne out as big, gentle horses and sturdy ponies help powerless kids to become empowered - helping those with a disability to develop abilities they scarcely imagined. On the back of a horse or special pony, the rider finds courage, strength and freedom.

A Little History on Us

By: Hollywood and Little Sugar
co-authored by Liz Vital

original Hollywood

original L'il Sugar

As you can tell from our story, *A Tale of Two Ponies*, life for us is pretty good.

In the modern era, 2010 to be exact we have it pretty much made. Walking around the arena with the loving volunteers and fun kids that come in to ride us is a breeze compared to what our Shetland pony ancestors endured. We've come a long way, baby.

Let us tell you a bit about our background.

We're very cute, as you know, but to be more specific we are the smallest of all horses. Our color usually alters based on the season, but the most common colors are black and dark brown. We often have irregular dark and white patches. There are four types of our Shetland breed: Classic, Modern, American and National Show Ponies.

Our great, great, great (great times one-hundred) grandparents were found running around the Shetland Isles, off the Northeast coast of Scotland around the 8th or 9th century. Small ponies on the Isles, originating from all the way back to the Bronze Age, were crossed with another small breed, the Dole Pony, brought in when the Norsemen invaded. That's how The Shetland Pony came to be!

Our relatives had long manes, tails and forelocks to protect them from the harsh, cold climate of Scotland. That's why we have such gorgeous features ourselves! Nowadays manes are more for good looks than for survival. We now spend our time trying to be the cutest ponies in the barn, but back in the old days and through the years the ponies had a lot more to worry about.

Despite our short stature, 9.3 to 10.2 hands, we are the strongest of all horses relative to our size. Our muscular legs and ability to work hard made us perfect in Scotland for carrying seaweed from the ocean for fertilizer and peat from the countryside to be used as fuel. Perhaps the hardest task our ancestors had to perform in the past was when the nineteenth century rolled around and brought with it the expansion of the coal industry. Not only were we used all over the United Kingdom to haul massive amounts of coal, but we were also imported to the United States. Sadly enough, some members of our families were dubbed "pit ponies." They were born and died in the mines and never even saw the light of day. Thank goodness machines eventually progressed so much that they didn't need us in the mines anymore once the 1900's came about.

Today we get to enjoy life for the most part and have fun. We have an innate driving ability and are sturdy and reliable animals for show and performance purposes. We also have sweet-natured personalities that make us great for carnivals, fair rides, personal pets and especially for our favorite job of all, equestrian therapy!

Shetland Ponies from Scotland

LIZ VITAL is the proud daughter of author and illustrator Linda Vital. Despite the fact that she had no choice in the matter she thoroughly believes that she was born with the most amazing mom in the entire world. Liz moved all over the country with her family and has settled in sunny Los Angeles for her current adult life. She has always had a love for writing and was thrilled when her mother asked her to be a part of this book. Liz is an actress, producer, fitness instructor and lover of life. She hopes that you enjoy this wonderful tale of two ponies.

Edwards Brothers Malloy
Thorofare, NJ USA
July 18, 2012